CECIL'S STORY

by George Ella Lyon

paintings by Peter Catalanotto

ORCHARD BOOKS   NEW YORK

A special thanks to Diane, Jim, Sophie, and especially Eli—P.C.

Text copyright © 1991 by George Ella Lyon
Illustrations copyright © 1991 by Peter Catalanotto

Orchard Books, A division of Franklin Watts, Inc.
387 Park Avenue South, New York, NY 10016

Manufactured in the United States of America. Printed by General Offset Company, Inc.
Bound by Horowitz/Rae. Book design by Mina Greenstein. The text of this book is set in
24 point Binny Old Style. The illustrations are watercolor paintings reproduced in full color.
10 9 8 7 6 5 4 3 2

Library of Congress Cataloging-in-Publication Data
Lyon, George Ella, date. Cecil's story / by George Ella Lyon ; paintings by
Peter Catalanotto.   p.   cm. Summary: A boy thinks about the possible scenarios that
exist for him at home if his father goes off to fight in the Civil War.
ISBN 0-531-05912-X.   ISBN 0-531-08512-0 (lib.)
[1. War—Fiction.   2. United States—History—Civil War, 1861–1865—Fiction.]
I. Catalanotto, Peter, ill.   II. Title.   PZ7.L9954Ce 1991 [E]—dc20   90-7775

In memory of my great-great-grandparents,
Esther and Adington Bruton,
and for Steve and Barbara

G.E.L.

For Nana and Papa

P.C.

If your papa went off to war,

he might get hurt

and your mama might go
to fetch him.

It might be a long journey,
so you'd have to stay with the neighbors.

You'd help look after their cows

and not cry till nighttime,
wiping your face on your shirttail.

If your papa was hurt bad,

your mama might stay for weeks
and not send word

because mail couldn't get through the fighting.
The neighbors would tell you that.
They would say to be brave.
But you'd wonder what would happen

if your papa should not come home

and you'd have to take care of Mama.

You'd know that you could do it—
chop wood, feed pigs and chickens.
You'd think about the plow, though.

How high were the handles?
Could you guide the mule and the plow, too,
if you put on the tallest boots?

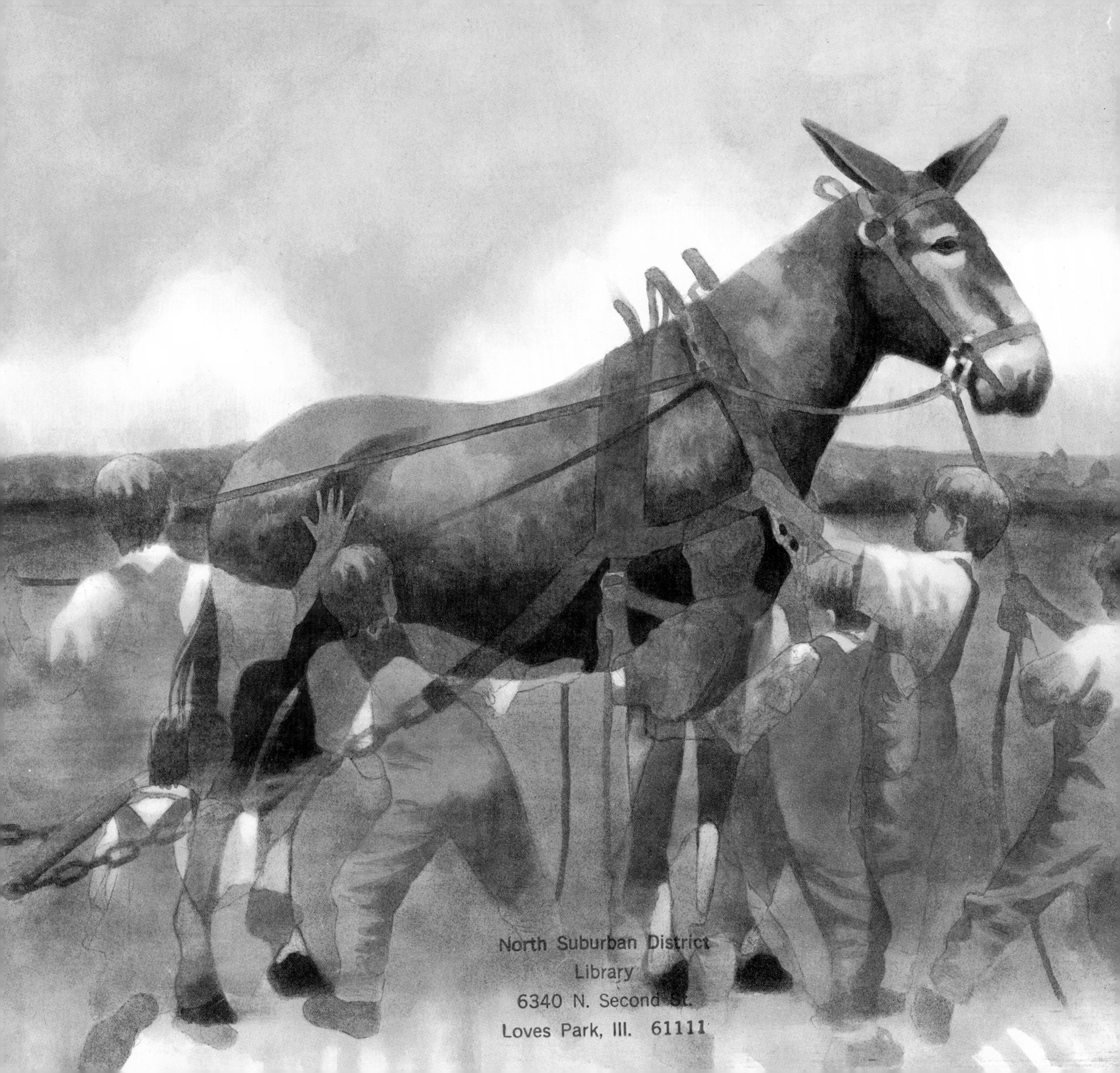

The neighbors would say not to worry.
Wounds take awhile to heal.
Your mama would be home by harvest.

If your papa went away to war

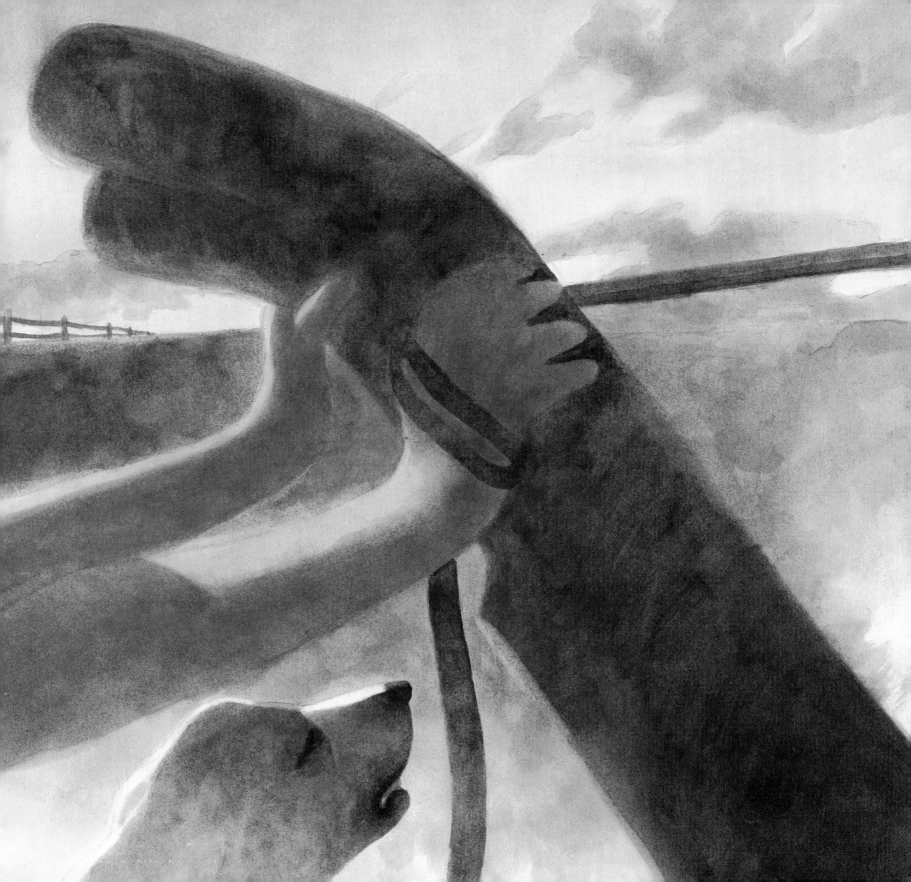

and came back with an arm missing,
or a leg, or he had a bad scar,
you wouldn't be afraid,
because you'd know he was still your papa—

the man who taught you before he left
to bait a hook and snare a rabbit,

the man strong enough to lift you now
with just one arm.